E
Gab

Gaban, Jesus
Tub time for Harry

DATE DUE		
NOV 7 - '92	JUL 2 0 1998	JUL. 0 2 2003
NOV 23 '92	JUL 2 9 199	APR. 2 0 2005
DEC 12 '92	OCT 1 0 199	AUG. 1 5 2005
JAN 2 '93	MAY 1 7 1999	AUG. 1 5 2005
JUL 17 '93	NOV 2 2 1999	OCT. 2 7 2005
SEP 8 - '93	DEC 0 6 199	FEB. 0 7 2005
JAN 17 '94	APR 2 2 2000	DEC 2 1 2012
FEB 5 '94	AUG 1 0 2000	MAR 0 8 2014
MAR 19 '94	SEP 3 2000	APR 1 4 2014
JUN 18 '94	MAR 0 5 2001	AUG 0 7 2017
AUG 26 '95	APR 1 6 2001	NOV 1 6 2018
OCT 28 '95	JUL 1 6 2001	
NOV 1 199	SEP 2 2 2001	MAR 3 0 2019

HARRY THE HIPPO

Tub Time for HARRY

By Jesús Gabán

Gareth Stevens Children's Books
MILWAUKEE

It's tub time for Harry.
He can hardly wait to
jump right in!

As Harry wriggles his toes,
his tub toys bob up and
down in the water.

Penny, Harry's favorite
tub-time toy, is even
dirtier than Harry!

4

"Just like new, Penny! Now
it's my turn to get clean!"

5

"Now that we're both
clean, let's have some
fun!" KERPLASH!

"Uh-oh! Now we've
done it! Let's clean
up this soapy mess!"

"Look, Penny. You can
see yourself in the tiles."

8

After all that work, Harry
needs a rest. He relaxes
in the warm, soapy tub...

9

. . . but not for long!
"Come on, Penny. It's
time to rinse off."

10

But the water comes out
too fast . "Careful, Penny!
I can't make it stop!"

Harry is scared. Water is
splashing everywhere.
"Help, Mama! Help!"

"Be careful, Mama! That
naughty hose is going
to get you, too!"

"What a mess, Harry.
There's more water
on the floor than in
the bathtub!"

14

"You're right, Mama. The
bathroom is a mess. But
Penny and I are clean!"

For a free color catalog describing Gareth Stevens' list of high-quality children's books, call 1-800-341-3569 (USA) or 1-800-461-9120 (Canada).

Library of Congress Cataloging-in-Publication Data

Gabán, Jesús.
   [Papouf prend son bain. English]
   Tub time for Harry / by Jesús Gabán. — North American ed.
      p. cm. — (Harry the hippo)
   Translation of: Papouf prend son bain.
   Summary: Little Harry tries a bath by himself but accidentally
loses control of the shower hose and gets water all over the bathroom.
   ISBN 0-8368-0718-9
   [1. Hippopotamus—Fiction. 2. Baths—Fiction.] I. Title. II. Series:
Gabán, Jesús. Harry the hippo.
PZ7.G1116Tu 1991
[E]—dc20   91-3218

North American edition first published in 1992 by

Gareth Stevens Children's Books
1555 North RiverCenter Drive, Suite 201
Milwaukee, Wisconsin 53212, USA

U.S. edition copyright © 1992. Text copyright © 1992 by Gareth Stevens, Inc.
First published in France, copyright © 1990 by Gautier-Languereau.

English text by Eileen Foran
Cover design by Beth Karpfinger and Sharone Burris

Printed in the United States of America

1 2 3 4 5 6 7 8 9 97 96 95 94 93 92